Preface

"A New Beginning" is a fiction story about social immorality behavior and its consequences. It focuses on one family and their surroundings. It took a terrible outcome for the head of the family to realize that they had hit rock bottom to change their ways and start over, this time, with love and respect as their banner.

Dedication

    I dedicate this fantastic work to Heidy, Efrain, Esther, and Esteban, my beloved children, who were the ones who had to put up with me every time I had an idea for the story and were happy to read it over and over until it was final. To my beloved husband Werner Pahnke for his love, support, and encouragement in finishing and publishing this story. I also want to dedicate this, my very first and hopefully not last inspiration, to Shirla Gonsalves, my loving and caring mother, "RIP," who gave me an excellent upbringing and taught me right from wrong and exceptional moral values. I love you and miss you, mom. Finally, to everyone who had something to do or say about this short story, your input is always highly appreciated. Thank you.

A new beginning

Nora was a beautiful17-year-old young lady who lived in an upscale neighborhood called San Bernardo. She is admired by her neighbors and friends for her beauty and criticized for her behavior. She was a real spoiled brat who only needed to open her mouth and demand when she wanted anything. If it was not granted, she would yell and throw an awful tantrum. She was still in the 8th grade because she hardly went to school, and when she did, it was mostly to hang out with her friends and do drugs in the washroom. Due to this behavior, she could not advance in school. Nora was street smart, but she was very lazy and hated studying when it came to school assignments.

Nora is the daughter of Brenda, the beautiful and hardworking wife of Victor Borrego, a co-owner of a successful company located on the outskirts of the city. As her parents nicknamed her, Norita is the only daughter of the couple. Soon after her 17th birthday, she met a boy who was also of her age. She thought he was very handsome. His nickname was Mono, and she did not really care to know his real name. He was new in the neighborhood; he was already a drunk and drug addict and had already robbed and vandalized the local convenience stores in the area. He wanted to establish his "bad boy" reputation, and he did a great job at that.

After hanging out with him for a couple of months, doing things she knew that she was not supposed to do like vandalizing personal properties of people she disliked, being cruel to her neighbors' pets, among other things, also create her "bad girl" profile, she found out she was pregnant. She did not want to tell her parents and was also worried that Mono would find out she knew that he was not the "daddy" type, so she did not say anything to anyone. For fear of losing her great figure before the eyes of her "nosey" neighbors and 'so-called friends who lived to criticize everything she did, but mostly because of the shame and embarrassment she knew that her condition would bring to her parents, she decided to wear girdles and bigger clothes to disguise her growing tummy until she could not bear the tightness anymore.

Although Nora was the proud spoiled brat of the neighborhood, she never thought of hurting her baby because it would be the fruit of her very first love. She was not planning on telling Mono about her pregnancy either because she thought he might either want her to have an abortion or lose interest in her, and she was unwilling to suffer any heartbreak.

She fled from home to go to live with her grandfather, who, in previous years, according to her mother, had sexually abused her and whom she hated with all her might, but she had nowhere else to go. Brenda was an only child, and her father was from Spain, so she had no other relatives in the country. Norita arrived at her grandfather's house at almost three in the morning. She knocked on the door so hard that the Old Man woke up scared and wondering what had happened. Norita kept banging on the door because she thought that he would be unconscious from the drunkenness he treated himself to every night, and she was not mistaking.

Gabriel woke up suddenly due to the banging on that door which caused him an instant headache. He opened the door with a bat in his hand, shirtless, wearing a pair of shorts and bare feet, ready to bring down the intruder of his dream. He was fairly young, but due to the life he lived, he seemed twice his age, his beard covered most of his face, his hair was long enough to touch his shoulders, and she could tell that his long hair was badly in need of some shampooing, his stomach seemed like of an 'eight-month pregnant' lady, all he did on a daily bases was sleep, spend quality time at the local bar drinking and smoking. When he opened the door and saw Norita, he dropped the bat and threw himself over her to hug her, but she was still so angry that her mother told her, avoiding the hug. She pushed him away from the door and walked in, heading towards the bedroom that belonged to her mother.

She shut the door behind her, and without saying a word, she went to sleep.

The next morning, she woke up to a familiar scent that brought back memories of when she was a little girl. As soon as she opened her eyes, she recognized the scent of bacon, scrambled eggs, and her favorite cornbread her grandparents made for her back in those days. Still, although she was dying to taste it again, her morning sickness due to the pregnancy did not allow her to do so. She ran into the restroom and threw up, then went out to the kitchen where Gabriel was, still excited to have his granddaughter home, however, not knowing what was going on in the young lady´s body or mind.

Gabriel had woken incredibly early to take a well-deserved and needed shower, shaved the beard, and combed his long-tangled hair. He now looked like the 58-year-old man he was, hoping that maybe his appearance last night is what Norita reacted to, but she walked into the kitchen and did not even say good morning. He tried

to talk to her a few times, but all she did was ignore the poor guy.

She walked towards the counter, picked up the plate she knew was

hers, and dropped it in the trash. He was shocked at her attitude and

asked for an explanation but got no answer in return; she walked out

of the kitchen back to her room still without saying a word. Gabriel

was discouraged and confused; his baby was there, but it was as if

she was a completely different person, and he did not know why. He

sat at the kitchen counter sobbing. He did not know what to think; all

he wanted was to hug her but did not even get a smile…

The days passed, and she woke up every morning to the fantastic

breakfast scent, had her favorite lunch ready for her at midday and

her favorite dinner every evening. Gabriel decided not to give up on

seeking reconciliation for whatever she thought had happened. At this point, Nora was confused and wondered if what her mother had told her was true. She decided to confront her grandfather by dressing in revealing clothing, flirting, and practically throwing herself at him, suggesting intercourse. Gabriel was terribly upset and confused; he scowled her and demanded an explanation.

For the first time in her life, a family member had raised their voice at her, so this was new and confusing to her, she felt rejected and insulted, but at the same time, she felt like someone cared... the first thing she said to him was… "my mother told me that you raped me when I was just a little girl, now that I´m grown, you reject me… I don´t get it" the poor old man almost got a heart attack when he heard that and denied that statement. Nora was embarrassed and did not know what to do with herself. For the first time in years, she sat and had a long talk and cried with her beloved grandfather. He explained his daughter's anger. She blamed him for her mother's death. ''You see"-he said... "my dear wife, your grandmother developed a heart condition; for years, we looked for help and spent a lot of money on specialists trying to find a cure. The treatment extended her life a little to the point that she could meet you and enjoy you for a few years. I witnessed my beloved wife grow ill and weaker as time passed, and I could not bear it anymore; I was extremely depressed and did not know what else to do; I was at the bar down the road more than I was here with her, trying to forget what she was going through. After all those years, we had been together, and death was right at the corner waiting to snatch her away from me, and it did not seem fair. Her illness so hurt me, and I did not take care of her as I should have; on the contrary, I immersed myself in liquor, and I regret that until this day.

When she died, I did not only lose my wife, but I also lost my daughter, who was still young, and my granddaughter I loved with all my heart. I cried day in and day out and begged God to allow me to join her. Luckily, he said no... I was so happy when I saw you at my door the other night. You look just like your mother at that age."

Nora was relieved and happy after listening to her grandfather's explanation, for she longed to have a sincere love in her life and someone who she could count on other than Mono. She stayed there until her baby was born, enjoying every moment and meal she missed for all those years. She even went to her prenatal appointments with her grandfather.

This created a bond between them again, and she decided to put aside what her mother told her. Knowing that it was not true, she understood her mother's pain, so she was not even upset with her. With the help of her grandfather, she stopped drinking, although she smoked but much less than before, they were working towards her quitting for good, but that took longer than the drinking. They went out for walks, for special dinners, Gabriel showed her off throughout the entire village, and everyone knew the beloved granddaughter who Gabriel so missed. One afternoon, late in her pregnancy, Nora had cravings for cheese, so Gabriel went to look for it in the kitchen; suddenly, he heard a scream, his granddaughter was ready to give birth, he took her to the hospital urgently and a beautiful girl was born. Despite all the time she was there, she did not tell her parents where she was and made the old man promise that he would never tell them. He agreed, although it did not seem right. He knew something was happening in the household because that behavior did not seem normal. His granddaughter was only 17 years old, the same age Brenda was when she became pregnant with Nora, so to him, it will not make sense that she would be upset with her daughter to the point of kicking her out for being pregnant. He questioned her about it, but all she told him was that she was old enough to know what she was doing and asked him to respect her privacy because she was not ready to talk about it. Gabriel agreed and did not continue asking.

The following day, since everything was fine with her and her daughter, they were discharged from the hospital. One night while he was asleep, Nora packed her things, wrote a letter apologizing for the way she acted at first, for leaving the way she did and leaving him in charge of her baby. She asked him to please register her as his daughter and give her all that love that she knows he had repressed. The baby girl was only a couple of weeks old, and Nora was recovered and ready to go home. She had enough time to think about how she lived her life and thought about changing her ways and studying to become a better person to return for her baby… at least those were her plans.

Nora was now 18 years old; She returned home, to school, to the boyfriend, and to the life she had before, only that she never dared to tell anyone about her daughter. Mono was so into himself that he did not even care that Norita was not around or where she disappeared to, he was not even aware of Nora's pregnancy. Twenty years went by, and she was still living with her parents; she did not finish her studies, and as for them (her parents), if she was happy and not lacking anything she wanted, even though she did not want to study or do anything for herself, it was fine. They still saw her as their baby girl, and she could do whatever she wanted whenever she wanted. She never knew what it was like to work or help with chores, she was with the same drug addict boyfriend and other friends with benefits that she had acquired over time and who visited her often, and neither Mono nor any of the others could say anything about it if they arrived. They found her with another or others.

One afternoon, Mono came to visit; she was alone since her mother, who was now the general manager of her company, was on vacation. Her father, who was now the sole owner of his, was on a business trip, as usual. That afternoon they got high until they passed out. Mono woke up before her and realized that Nora was totally gone and was not reacting to anything; he got scared and called the paramedics, who arrived shortly after the call. She was rushed to the hospital, where she underwent several tests due to the overdose and her sexual behavior reported by Mono. As a result of the exams, she was diagnosed with HIV and AIDS, Mono and her other special friends also had to be tested, and they all were infected; no one knew who brought the virus to the group. Mono, the day after receiving the news, decided to end his life because it was not worth living for him.

Nora, as usual, did not say anything to her parents, but now she was willing to change, continue with her treatments and follow her doctor's orders. With Mono out of the picture, she had a chance to succeed, and so she remained sober and drug-free for several more years. On the other hand, Brenda continued in her wanderings, year after year. She took vacations when she knew that her husband would have to be on his business trips to spend time on the farm of one of her lovers. During her vacation getaway, she received a message from Nora informing her that she was undergoing a special treatment session at the hospital and that she would probably be back in about two days. Nora knew that she was in her final stage. However, Brenda had not realized that her daughter was so sick and that this was her way of saying goodbye forever.

When Brenda received the strange message from Nora, she told her lover about it. Knowing the kind of woman that Norita had become, he convinced her to spend the night with him, and that he would take her to the hospital early the next day, Brenda who was so into this man, agreed to stay with him that night. The next morning, interrupting their vacation, he took Brenda to visit her daughter at the hospital as per the message "for her treatment" mistakenly, she entered the maternity ward, where she heard the heartrending cries of a young woman in labor. The voice seemed so familiar to her that she had to see who it was; she peeked through the glass on the door and saw the young woman who was in great pain. However, despite the pain, she reflected on her face and voice did not lose her beauty.

Brenda thought to herself: "Wow, what a beautiful girl, her voice and her face remind me of someone," she tried for a moment to remember the face of her friends and the people close to her but could not identify who she reminded her of. With the girl's face imprinted on her mind, she left that room and went to meet her daughter. Upon arriving at her destination, she found them cleaning and disinfecting the room, she asked about her daughter, and they gave her the news that her daughter had died the night before.

Upon receiving the news, she refused to believe it and demanded to talk to the doctor or the person in charge immediately. Although she

was in misbelieve, she could not avoid the tears and the fright of

losing her baby; the nurse got a chair and helped her take a seat,

and brought her a glass of water while someone got the doctor for

her.

When the doctor walked in, she became angry and frustrated and

even blamed him for killing her baby, she even tried to get

aggressive, but the doctor understood her reaction and hugged her

until he could calm her down. He then spoke and explained that he

had been treating her daughter for 5 years. Brenda could not believe

what she was hearing. She had never realized that her daughter was

a drug addict, much less that she had HIV and AIDS. She asked why

no one had informed her about anything. He replied, saying... "Nora

did not want to interrupt your schedule, your daughter preferred not to say anything because you were always too busy with work, and she did not want to be a burden to her parents; she was entitled to her privacy after all," he also told her that despite the orders of Nora, he left several messages on her answering machine at home and voice messages on her cell phone. For a week now, he was trying to locate her. At that point, Brenda realized that his attempts to locate her would be in vain because she was at the house of one of her special friends for those two weeks while her husband was on a business trip and would not return for another two weeks.

She asked to see her daughter since she had not seen her for almost 15 days. They took her to the hospital morgue. A cold and metallic place, they pulled the lifeless body out of the cooler on a metal sheet; Brenda held her lifeless daughter in her arms, hugged her very tight, begging for forgiveness. She cried again; this time convinced of her disgrace. She asked for forgiveness because after talking to the doctor, she realized that throughout Norita's life, she only gave her what she asked for, there was little to no conversation between them, they never went out to do mother-daughter things and thinking things through, she did not remember having even scolded her for anything ever, not for the time he had escaped from home for a little over 5 months or for leaving her studies and much less for the number of boyfriends and girlfriends she brought home. She felt guilty for giving her that much liberty to live as she chose.

Being there with her daughter, she stared at her and spoke knowing that she would not receive an answer; she combed her daughter's hair with her fingers, until then, she realized how emaciated and skinny her little girl looked; however, she noticed the incredible resemblance to the young woman she had recently seen in the delivery room. She stayed a while longer contemplating her beloved Norita, realizing that in life, she had not spent as much time with her as she is doing now because of her husband, work, studies, friends, and boyfriends. A morgue worker arrived to tell her that her time was up. Brenda walked out visibly affected without saying anything.

Arriving at the hospital's exit, she saw her father, whom she had not seen for almost 40 years. Gabriel, who could hardly walk without a cane, did not recognize his daughter at first sight, but when Brenda saw him, she hugged him tightly and once again cried inconsolably; her father, who had no idea what was happening, remained silent, embracing his daughter who he missed so much when Brenda calmed down, she asked her father the reason for his presence in the hospital. Still, before he could answer, she asked him to please not tell her that he was sick because she could not bear another bad news on the same day.

At that point, a tall and handsome young man approached them; he seemed in a hurry, so without hesitation, and interrupting their conversation, he said, "come on, dad, I want to see my baby" Brenda thought it was strange that this young man called her father dad, so she inquired. Gabriel introduced her to the young pilot as his beloved daughter, the young man instead of shaking hands, hugged her very tight and said: "you are as beautiful as her," this comment confused Brenda even more, but before she could react, her father interrupted by suggesting them to enter the hospital, since he knew that she had no idea about Nora's daughter. When she arrived at the maternity ward, Brenda demanded that her father explain what was happening. He sighed and then took her to the cafeteria while Pedro went in to see his wife and newborn baby.

When they arrived at the café, Gabriel asked Norita, and she told him about her grief. Upon hearing the story, the abandoned grandfather and father also became sad; after drying his tears, he thought it would be a good time to tell his daughter about that time, years ago, when Nora spent a few months at home. Brenda could not believe what she was hearing. In a single day and through the mouths of others, she learned that her daughter was as promiscuous as she was, she was addicted to drugs, she was sick with HIV and AIDS, she had given birth to a baby girl whom she abandoned, and that she was also dead. Her father told her about the attitude of his granddaughter when she arrived and how things changed little by little between them. Of course, Brenda felt guilty because she had planted that senseless hatred in her daughter for no reason.

She explained to her father that she was very hurt by her mother's death and the attitude he adopted regarding that situation by immersing himself in alcohol. She told him that Norita did not understand why they had moved from his village so suddenly and far from her grandfather, who she loved so much, that she did not want to be far from him and would not stop asking for him, she was suffering and that is why she told her that. Crying, Brenda begged her father to forgive her. He understood her explanation and forgave her without hesitation. After all, he knew that that was the reason for all this confusion. Something in her heart told her that Norita did not die with that hatred towards her grandfather; as for Gabriel, he knew that when Norita left his house leaving her baby girl, she was convinced that this terrible accusation from her mother was not true. Gabriel held the hands of his daughter and, looking straight into her eyes, and he said: "I assure you that there was no hatred in her heart," he told her of the tenderness and intelligence of his granddaughter and the ability she had to analyze situations. Right then and there, Brenda understood that she had completely ignored her daughter throughout her life. Still, now, she wanted to see her granddaughter immediately, whom her father named Nora in honor of the mother she never saw. As they walked through the corridors on the way to her room, she thought of what she would say to her, and she was visibly nervous and anxious. However, when arriving at the door, she stopped to think about the reaction of that young woman and began asking her father… "what do I do if she rejects me? What if she blames me because her mother abandoned her?" But Gabriel reassured her that it would be fine. He trusted the education he had given his Norita.

When Nora, his granddaughter, went away, leaving him with the baby, he determined in his heart to change and give her everything

he had not given Brenda, his own daughter. Gabriel sought help with

a psychologist to know how to supply all his great-granddaughter's

needs since before the baby began to walk and talk, he left his vices

that were smoking and drinking, he joined a local church, stopped

dating women, and dedicated his entire life to enjoy the second

opportunity that God gave him to raise who would now be his

reason for living, his second chance. Nora went to the best school in

the village and participated in church activities. She always was and

is active in the community. She graduated with honors from the

university, and she met Pedro, who is also active in the church; they

have been married for two years, and now they have their baby girl.

Upon hearing all this, Brenda felt envious for not knowing what to do

with her daughter, and now, more than before, she was deeply sorry for having left her father, who could have given her good advice for the upbringing of her Nora. Gabriel hugged his daughter and told her that it is not too late to win her granddaughter's love and recover her self-esteem and husband's love. Gabriel, hearing what his beloved granddaughter's life had been like, was more than certain that his son-in-law was not on a business trip but with another woman and suggested that before leaving the hospital, she should call him. She agreed, and they went to meet Nora and her granddaughter, both for the first time.

Arriving in the room, Brenda realized that she saw the same young woman in pain before she reached Norita's room; she looked at her. Without saying a word, the young woman extended her arms, asking for a hug; they had not met before. Still, her grandfather made sure to create a loving memory of her mother and grandparents in

Norita's mind and heart because he always knew that they would show up sooner or later. Brenda hugged her back tightly and started to cry, this time of joy, she asked Norita if she knew who she was, she answered: "Yes, you are my grandmother, I was waiting on you, Pedro had already told me that he ran into you and I was eager to meet you" Nora pointed to her baby's crib and said: "There is your great-granddaughter" Brenda said: "I still do not know you, but I love you with all my might," she turned to her father and said, "thank you, dad."

She got up and walked towards her great-granddaughter's crib while asking for the baby's name: Nora replied: "Genesis, for a new beginning for everyone" Brenda said: "Excellent, for a new beginning, and a new opportunity." She gently hugged the baby for a while, kissed her forehead, and gave her to Pedro, who she also hugged tenderly. Gabriel reminded her of a call she had to make, so she said goodbye to her new family members with a tender kiss for each one and left the room with her dad at her side. At this point, Brenda was warm-hearted and feeling like part of something great called family. She had her own but was never able to feel that way... she completely spoiled her daughter, and the relationship between her and her husband was only based upon appearance and great sex. When leaving the room, Brenda searched for a public telephone as instructed by Gabriel so that Victor will not identify the phone number and called him. The phone rang. He answered, it turns out that he was not traveling, Brenda told him about Norita and where she was, Victor was speechless for a moment while he absorbed the news then began to cry, on the other side of the phone, Brenda could hear the worrying voice of a woman asking what is wrong before he hung up the call.

In less than half an hour, he was at the hospital. He went to see his Norita with Brenda, while the three of them were in that cold and frightening place, both confessed in front of their daughter's lifeless body and promised to fight for their marriage and for the second opportunity that God had given them to have a normal family, now with their granddaughter's family and Gabriel. He never agreed with Brenda's attitude by abandoning her father that way, and he even tried to persuade her several times to visit him. However, she was still very hurt and did not assimilate forgiveness for her father without thinking about her pain because she lost the only woman she loved from her childhood.

They left the morgue, and Brenda took him to see his granddaughter Nora, her husband Pedro, and great-granddaughter Genesis, who also represented a new beginning for him. It was difficult for them to return home, knowing that Norita would not return. The neighbors who knew Nora's adventures were already speaking about her death, the funeral was the next day, Brenda, Victor, Nora, Pedro, and Gabriel attended. Brenda and Victor took the lifeless body of Norita to her grandfather's village for the funeral. A place where those who knew her loved her, and for them, she would rest in peace there and not in the cemetery of her community because of the "bad girl" reputation that little by little they were getting to know about their beloved daughter.

A few months later, Brenda submitted her resignation, and Victor only went to the office when it was indispensable. They sold their house and bought an apartment close to Gabriel, who could not move around freely without his cane but was lucid and knew everything around him and Nora. They were able to dedicate quality time to their granddaughter and great-granddaughter. They enjoyed Gabriel's company for a couple more years, then buried him next to his wife and Norita. Each year of Norita's death anniversary, they visit her place of Rest, and the next day they threw a huge party to celebrate the birthday of Genesis. On her fourth birthday, Nora announced that she was pregnant, this time with twins, which brought even more joy to the family. Of course, they were sad that grandpa was no longer with them, but they knew that he was resting in peace. Nora and Pedro no longer had the help of Gabriel, but in his place, their grandparents were there to support, pamper and be with the babies paying close attention to each of them and realizing everything they had missed while Nora was growing.

It was definitely… A new beginning…